THE ARDOR OF AN ARCHITECT

BEYOND THE ARISTOCRACY

LINDA RAE SANDE

Twisted Teacup
PUBLISHING

BLURB

She kissed an architect. A witness says otherwise. The gossip is building faster than he can design a house.

When a woman from his past unexpectedly kisses architect Daniel Sinclair in his office, he finds himself unwittingly thrust into the spotlight of Edinburgh's gossip scene. The news spreads swiftly, thanks in large part to his secretary, who witnessed the intimate moment. As a result, Daniel is branded a rogue, a reputation he'd much rather shake off in favor of being recognized for his cutting-edge house designs.

Meanwhile, seamstress Isabella Farnsworth is forced to leave her childhood home and seeks refuge in Edinburgh. She has friends in the city, including one whom she nostalgically recalls from their carefree days at his grandparents' estate in Derbyshire. However, she never intended for her presence to stir up rumors of impropriety that could lead to a proposal of marriage from him.

Though she harbors a secret desire to marry Daniel, Isabella yearns for their union to be built on genuine affection. How can a woman truly discern if a man loves her?

ALSO BY LINDA RAE SANDE

The Daughters of the Aristocracy

The Kiss of a Viscount

The Grace of a Duke

The Seduction of an Earl

The Sons of the Aristocracy

Tuesday Nights

The Widowed Countess

My Fair Groom

The Sisters of the Aristocracy

The Story of a Baron

The Passion of a Marquess

The Desire of a Lady

The Brothers of the Aristocracy

The Love of a Rake

The Caress of a Commander

The Epiphany of an Explorer

The Widows of the Aristocracy

The Gossip of an Earl

The Enigma of a Widow

The Secrets of a Viscount

The Widowers of the Aristocracy

The Dream of a Duchess

The Vision of a Viscountess

The Conundrum of a Clerk

The Charity of a Viscount

The Cousins of the Aristocracy

The Promise of a Gentleman

The Pride of a Gentleman

The Holidays of the Aristocracy

The Christmas of a Countess

The Knot of a Knight

The Holiday of a Marquess

The Snow Angel of a Duke

The Ivy of an Earl

The Heirs of the Aristocracy

The Angel of an Astronomer

The Puzzle of a Bastard

The Choice of a Cavalier

The Bargain of a Baroness

The Jewel of an Earl's Heir

The Vixen of a Viscount

The Honor of an Heir

The Rose of a Sultan's Son

The Ladies of the Aristocracy

The Lady of a Grump

The Lady of a Sultan

The Pursuit of a Duchess

The Lords of the Aristocracy

The Abduction of an Earl

Beyond the Aristocracy

The Pleasure of a Pirate

The Making of a Mistress

The Bride of a Baronet

The Caton of a Captain

Puss and Pots

The Betrothal of a Baron

Masquerade Meow

The Grand Tours of the Aristocracy

A Courtship in Catania

An Affaire in Athens

A Lover in Luxor

A Rogue in Rome

Revenge of the Wallflowers

The Wager of a Wallflower

Stella of Akrotiri

Origins

Deminon

Diana

The Lyon's Den (Dragonblade Publishing)

The Courage of a Lyon

The Lady of a Lyon

The Loyalty of a Lyon

The Librarian of a Lyon

Note: Translations of select titles are available in German, Italian, Spanish and Portuguese.

CHAPTER 1
A MOST UNEXPECTED KISS

he office of D. Sinclair, Architect, New Town, Edinburgh, Scotland, 1832

Daniel Sinclair waited as the newcomer entered his office, expecting her to openly gawk at him. All the women did. Some of the men, too, as if he were an animal in the menagerie at the Tower of London and was there to be admired.

He had a thought he should charge admission.

Some were quick to turn away, their faces heating with blushes, but others could not help themselves, their mouths gaping as they openly stared at him.

Had they no shame? No self-control?

He couldn't help that he was excessively handsome. That his parents had both been attractive and perfectly suited to one another. That his dark hair was wavy and possessed of a forelock that seemed to curl at precisely the right location on his forehead without any assistance from him. That he was blessed—or cursed—with sapphire eyes and a square jaw, a set of eyebrows whose dark hairs didn't jut off in unfortunate directions, and a nose void of a hook.

Even his mother was prone to sigh with self-satisfaction upon seeing him. That happened every Sunday when he paid a call at Sinclair House for dinner. Although his father was getting on in years, he still retained his handsome features despite his hair having grayed until it was nearly white. His mother was similarly blessed, although her brunette hair had yet to display a single strand of gray.

Or perhaps it had, and she was merely plucking them out.

Ouch!

His involuntary shudder reminded him he had a visitor. She was exactly where his secretary, Arthur Peabody, had left her only the moment before, which meant she was standing just inside his office—not far enough over the threshold to close the door on her, but not exactly *in* the office, either.

Well, the bell skirt of her gown was mostly in the office the gathers of the yellow fabric rounding out well beyond the width of her natural hips in an effort to compete with sleeves so puffy, they might have been hiding arms capable of tossing a caber. At least they were tight around her forearms. He couldn't be sure any other part of the gown was fitted given the lacy shawl wrapped around her shoulders.

Who designed such awful garments for women? They should be found guilty of deliberate sabotage against a woman's natural beauty and be sentenced to gaol. When he was younger—probably ten or so—he distinctly remembered his mother and all her friends wearing gowns reminiscent of those worn by the Greek goddesses. The frocks flattered every figure and made all women appear as if they, too, were goddesses.

He tried to imagine the rather pretty woman wearing such a gown and found the image far more pleasing. In fact, now that he had a chance to study her more closely, he realized she was older than he had first thought, but not matronly in any sense of the word.

Her blonde hair was swept up into a coiffure that was partly hidden by the straw hat she wore at a jaunty angle, its brim on one side liberally festooned with silk flowers. Her yellow gown—*jonquil*, he corrected himself—seemed to lighten his office despite the unusually large size of the window behind him.

A large window only helped light his office if the sky beyond it wasn't gray with impending rain.

Intending to look for a wedding band, Daniel glanced at her hands. Both were ensconced in white cotton gloves. If she wore any rings, they were hidden.

When he raised his gaze back up to her face, he gave a start.

She wasn't staring at him, exactly. In fact, she seemed mildly amused, and he was struck by the thought that she knew his deepest, darkest secret and mayhap intended to use it against him for some nefarious purpose.

He could not for the life of him think of what that secret might be, though. Yet, here she was, grinning at him, an elegant blonde brow arched as if she did indeed know that very secret.

"I wondered if I'd find you here in town," she said, poised as if to curtsy.

He hadn't bothered to bow, mostly because his mind was still on the project he had begun designing, and her arrival had interrupted an epiphany that had him realizing exactly how it could be built with sandstone, faced with brick, and stucco'd to appear as if it were made of marble.

He would design it in a sort of Greek Revival style featuring Palladian windows. The roof would have to be of slate, of course, but he could make it work if the windows were trimmed in black. Surely his client would agree once he saw the elevation drawings. If necessary, he could always do a sketch in perspective and then enhance it with watercolor paints. He knew most clients required that extra step to help them visualize how their building might look when it was completed to his specifications.

Yes, that's exactly what he would do.

He almost retook his seat at the drafting table to resume his work, but the scent of lemons drifted past his nostrils and he once again remembered he had a visitor.

"I'm... I'm afraid you have me at a disadvantage," he said stepping from behind his drafting table to regard her with a quirked brow.

"Oh, I rather doubt that," she said, her grin widening into a smile. "It's very good to see you again, Daniel."

His eyes narrowing, he studied her for a moment. "Uh..." He swallowed as she approached, and he managed not to grunt when she placed a hand against the side of his torso as if for support, stood on tiptoes, and kissed him, first on one cheek and then the other. Quite a feat given the hat she wore, and yet, never once did the brim touch his face.

Daniel blinked.

Now this had never happened before. No woman had ever simply entered his office and kissed him in the middle of the day. In fact, other than his mother, no woman had ever kissed him. Even his secretary, who was watching them from beyond his open office door, seemed shocked. The young man's eyes widened before he quickly returned his attention to the papers on his desk.

Serves him right for not minding his own business. My business, Daniel thought.

The scents of honeysuckle and lemon drifted past his nose, bringing with them a jumble of memories from summers spent down in Derbyshire at his maternal grandparents' estate. They did not, however, bring a memory of *her*.

Lowering her half-boots to the wooden floor-boards, she regarded him with that same knowing grin before she suddenly sobered. "You don't recognize me, do you?" she asked in dismay.

"Uh..." He shook his head. This was surely some sort of setup. An arrangement made to interrupt his work on the McDonald project. Although he had a verbal assurance from the judge to do the design, he didn't yet have the contract. It was possible he was up against only one other architect for the job. Wilkins didn't have the vision necessary for a post-Georgian era building in New Town, though. The old codger did better at the few restorations being done in the medieval Old Town of Edinburgh.

Daniel chuckled softy at the thought she might be a lady of the evening hired by his friend, Watson, to embarrass him. "Watson put you up to this, didn't he?" he asked. "How much did he pay you?"

The woman arched the blonde brow again, but her

expression lost all its humor. "You really don't remember me," she whispered.

Daniel swallowed. Perhaps she was an actress. Yes, that would be just like Watson to hire an actress to embarrass him in the middle of his workday, in front of his secretary, who he was quite sure preferred the company of men to women and probably only worked for him because he was such a handsome example of a mortal man.

Before he could respond to the woman's comment, he noted how for the briefest of moments, a look of disappointment crossed her face. Or was that anger? Mayhap tinged with a bit of... dare he think it? Evil?

"Then I suppose I must make an effort to leave you with the very best first impression," she said.

Before Daniel knew quite what was happening, she placed both gloved hands on his shoulders, stood on tiptoes, and kissed him on the lips.

He was so stunned, he didn't respond at first. Except he did open his mouth, because, well, wouldn't anyone who was shocked? The sensation of such soft pillows pressed to his lips was so pleasing, so unexpected, he inhaled softly and discovered exactly what made a kiss so enjoyable.

The suckling sensation was quite addictive. So much so, he returned the kiss in equal measure, angling his head slightly in an effort to better fit his lips to hers. Ten degrees... no, make that a fifteen degree tilt of his head, and their lips were perfectly locked. As for what to do next, his hands seemed to know before he did, capturing her waist on either side despite the distant thought that his fingertips were nearly black with the Cumberland graphite from the pencil he used to do his architectural drawings. The yellow fabric would be stained with his fingerprints.

Well, it would serve her right, invading his office in the middle of a workday and behaving as if she were a rake.

Or would that be *rakette*?

He couldn't be too upset with her, though, even if she was an actress. This kissing was rather enjoyable, as was the sensation of one gloved hand smoothing down the side of his waistcoat. He hoped her fingers wouldn't discover the opening in the side seam where the thread had broken. He didn't wear a topcoat whilst he worked at his drafting table, and his shirt sleeves were rolled up to his elbow to keep them from becoming smeared with graphite.

Dammit. Her forefinger had caught in the hole just as her palm reached his hip. He heard a sound and realized he had made it in the back of his throat.

A warning sound, as if part of him—the sane-and-never-been-kissed part of him—knew what was to happen next.

The I'm-enjoying-this-kiss-and-how-dare-you-stop-me part of him tried to ignore it. That is, until her gloved hand flattened over the front of his pantaloons in an area that had suddenly grown tight.

The I'm-enjoying-this-kiss-and-how-dare-you-stop-me part of him lost its battle when he jerked back, breaking off the kiss—and her contact down below—leaving him to blink several times in disbelief.

He stared down at her, his shock slowly abating as he considered what he should do next, especially when he saw how her eyes were slightly glazed, her lips red and swollen, her cheeks pink with warmth.

He had half a mind to start the kiss again, but the thought of what she would tell Watson had him reconsidering.

He should throw her out of his office, of course. Lift her over his shoulder and unceremoniously dump her on the settee he had purchased for the outer office in an effort to make his business appear more legitimate. Scold her for her impertinence—didn't she have a better way to make her living than kissing unsuspecting gentlemen in their places of business? Perhaps acting didn't pay very well, but that didn't mean she could simply interrupt his workday and kiss him without warning.

"How much did he pay you?" he asked.

It was her turn to blink. "Pay me?" she repeated, her voice sounding breathy. "Whatever are you talking about?" Her attention had gone to his waistcoat, and he saw how one of her blonde brows furrowed as she once again pressed a finger to the open edge of the superfine wool.

Apparently she had noticed the hole in his side seam, not hard given her finger had been caught in it only the moment before.

"Watson. How much did he pay you to come in here and... and kiss me?"

Her brows rose in unison as a look of delight appeared to lighten her features. "No one *paid* me, you idiot," she said, pulling her hand away from his waistcoat. "If you're still friends with that ne'er-do-well, then you would already know he's too Scotch to pay for anything."

Daniel gave a start. It was true. Callum Watson wasn't a spendthrift.

"But I did wonder how long you would allow it," she said, angling her head as she sighed. "Apologies, *sir*. Apparently I've taken up too much of your time. Perhaps we can continue this reunion when you're not at your place of employment." Without another word, she dipped a slight curtsy and took her leave.

A look of disappointment crossing his face, Daniel watched her go. Although her bell skirt hid the true width of her hips, it certainly accentuated the movement of them as she walked, and his nether region, barely recovered from when she had pressed her hand against it, reacted once again.

Reunion?

Apparently, the woman in yellow was someone from his past. Someone who also knew Watson.

The realization dawned at the same time he noticed Arthur openly staring at him. Or was he staring at his nether region? It took all his self-control not to cover his crotch with his hands.

Pulling back his shoulders and displaying a look suggesting someone might come to bodily harm in the next minute, Daniel said, "No more callers today, Peabody."

"Yes, sir," Arthur replied, a finger hooked into his cravat so as to loosen it. "Very well, sir."

Daniel returned to his drafting table and resumed his work on the McDonald project.

Perhaps instead of a faux marble exterior, he would suggest it be painted the color of jonquils. He shook his head as if to clear it of a memory from his childhood in Derbyshire and was soon engrossed in drawing.

CHAPTER 2
CHILDHOOD
FRIENDS REUNITE

*M*eanwhile, in George Street near Charlotte Square

Opening her umbrella against the sudden downpour that seemed to time itself to the exact moment she exited the architect's office, Isabella Farnsworth wondered why she bothered.

Tears had already begun streaming down her face, several dripping onto her shawl. She fished a handkerchief from her pocket and quickly dabbed at her cheeks while she glanced both left and right.

"Watson, where are you?" she whispered, sniffling.

"Did he see you?"

Isabella gave a start, whirling around to discover Callum Watson standing on the threshold of a coffee house. He waved to indicate she should enter the establishment, and she quickly closed her umbrella and ducked inside. "You frightened me," she scolded.

"Apologies. I waited for you outside, but then it started to rain," he complained, motioning to one of the few available tables. With the gloomy weather, the coffee house was more crowded than usual. He held a chair for her and she sat, hoping he didn't notice she had been crying.

"I saw him," she said, glad when a waiter approached their table with pencil and pad in hand. She said, "Tea, please, with milk. And a biscuit."

"Millefruit, Dutch, or butter?"

She glanced over at Callum. "One of each," she replied.

"Coffee for me," Callum said, before the waiter could ask.

After the waiter hurried off, Isabella regarded her childhood friend with a wan grin and sighed. "Well, he's still incredibly handsome," she said.

"I warned you," he replied, waving his hands at his sides.

"He didn't recognize me."

Callum gave a start and suddenly crossed his arms. "Did you give your name?"

She shook her head. "No. But I left my calling card with his secretary. He seemed to think *you* put me up to some sort of act to embarrass him."

Callum blinked. "Why would he assume that?" he asked in confusion.

Isabella thought it best not to admit what she had done. She hadn't exactly planned to kiss Daniel. She hadn't thought to embarrass him, or to leave him with a poor impression of her. She had only meant to reenact one of her memories of their time together as children.

Not that she had ever actually kissed him back then, although it had *almost* happened. And she surely hadn't touched him as she had a few minutes ago. She wasn't even sure what had possessed her to slide her hand down the side of his body like that.

Well, that wasn't exactly true. She had noticed the odd spot in the side seam of his waistcoat and thought to discover if it needed repair.

Despite the cotton gloves she wore, poking her forefinger into the hole allowed her to feel his firm torso and the top of his hip, and to determine the thread of the waistcoat seam had merely broken. A few minutes with a needle and thread, and it would be fixed, good as new.

She had only pressed her palm against his arousal because the knuckle of her forefinger had been caught in the seam when she tried to pull it out, so her hand had no where else to go.

The feel of the hard ridge of his manhood beneath her fingers had been unnerving.

Unexpected.

For some reason, it had been thrilling, though. To know that he—or at least his body—could be aroused in her presence.

Even if he didn't know who she was.

The thought had a sob robbing her of breath. She tried to swallow the lump in her throat and failed.

"There's no need to cry."

Isabella stared at Callum, her first thought that he was terribly out of focus. She blinked several times, which sent tears cascading down her cheeks. "I didn't know I was," she murmured.

The waiter appeared with their order. When he placed her tea on the table, he noticed her wet cheeks and directed a censorious glare at Callum before slamming his coffee in front of him.

"Hey, it's not *my* fault," Callum said, before the waiter stalked off.

"He didn't recognize me," Isabella said softly.

"What did you say?"

"Daniel didn't recognize me," she repeated. "I thought sure if I wore a yellow gown, he would know it was me."

Pouring milk into his coffee, Callum dipped his head. "Well, in his defense, Izzy, you don't look like you used to," he said. When she expressed confusion, he added, "Well, your face is clean, as is your dress," he added. "You used to look as if you..." He paused. "Rolled in the dirt," he finished lamely.

"That's because I slept on the floor of our cottage. The *dirt* floor," she said on a sigh. "I was too young to know any better. Father never told us to wash up in the morning."

"You didn't have a looking glass?" he teased.

She was suddenly back in the cottage in Tideswell, glancing into her parent's room. Her father had kept it exactly as it was when her mother was alive, her dressing table still adorned with her comb, hairbrush, and cosmetics. Isabella might have used the mirror above the dressing table if her father hadn't forbidden her from entering the small bedchamber. "I didn't have one," she admitted. But it's not as if we grew up poor, because we weren't—"

"Your clothing suggested otherwise," he interrupted.

"Father didn't know how to be a mother," she murmured.

Callum nodded his understanding. "Truth be told, I didn't recognize you at first, either," he admitted, before lifting the coffee cup to his lips. "You're... pretty now. As is your gown."

Isabella sniffled. "Thank you, I think," she replied, stirring her tea. "I made the gown. I'm a seamstress, and I am hoping there is more work for me here in Edinburgh than there was in Tideswell." As for why she hadn't remained in England and moved to one of the cities there—she had considered York—she discovered she wouldn't be allowed to do her own banking without the assistance of a male relative. In Scotland, she could open an account and access her funds on her own, although it was recommended she at least be in the company of a man when she did so.

She had thought to ask Daniel if he might be that man, but their brief reunion hadn't gone as planned. Any thought of blunt and banking had fled her head at the mere sight of him.

Did women in Edinburgh fall prostrate at his feet and beg him for his attentions? Bow as he passed them on the street, treating him as if he were a god?

He could probably set up an exhibit featuring only him in Inverleith Park and charge admission!

She pushed the plate of biscuits in Callum's direction. "Would you like one?"

"I would," he replied. "Thank you." He took the Dutch biscuit and ate half of it in one bite.

"Daniel thought you employed me to pay a call on him. He thought I was an actress."

Callum scoffed softly before eating the rest of his biscuit. "As if I have the funds for such an endeavor," he said, grinning.

"I told him he was an idiot for thinking it," she went on, watching to see how her childhood friend would react.

She wasn't disappointed when he pretended offense before he chuckled. "Did you really call him an idiot?"

Nodding, she took a sip of tea. The warm liquid seemed to settle her nerves as well as clear her throat. "Do you see him often?"

He lifted a shoulder. "A couple of times a week, I suppose. We take our supper at one of the pubs over in Rose Street," he explained. "Although there is a new one we're going to try in a day or two."

"It's so good you two are still friends," she remarked.

"He's a good sport to put up with me," Callum replied. "He, an architect with eight projects already built, one in process, another on the drafting table, and me, a mere clerk at a warehouse," he added. "You never did say why it was you came to Edinburgh," he commented. "Although it is a nice surprise. I suppose you got my address from my mum?"

"I did," she admitted. "She says you don't write often enough, and I'm supposed to scold you, so consider yourself scolded."

He bobbed his head up and down. "Message noted. But that's not the only reason you came up here," he prompted.

"Father died," she stated.

Callum's eyes rounded, and he quickly sobered.

"I'm so sorry. I... I didn't know," he murmured. "Must have been recently?"

Isabella thought the comment odd and said, "Only a few months ago, actually," she replied, her cheeks burning when she remembered she wasn't wearing black. Only two modistes in town knew her, but neither had asked about her situation when they met with her about taking on sewing projects.

"Mum didn't mention it in her last letter," Callum replied, once again dipping his head. "You're not wearing black."

She ignored the comment. "Charlie has taken over the mercantile," she stated, referring to her younger brother, "and he married a girl from Buxton. Only a day before Father died."

"Charlie is *married*?" Callum asked in disbelief. "Oh. For some reason I thought he would always be a bache—"

"He no longer looks as if he rolls in the dirt, either," she interrupted. "In fact, he's quite an amiable young man. Said I should send his regards. Since Father's death, he, uh, he's had some work done to the cottage. Added a real floor and decent furnishings," she explained. "Made it quite a comfortable home."

Isabella once again remembered her parents' bedchamber. She had managed to take the hairbrush and comb from the dressing table before her brother's renovations, determined they not become the property of her sister-in-law.

"So... you're still living there?" he guessed.

She shook her head. "No. Now that he's married, my presence is no longer... required," she stammered. "His wife can see to the household now, and..."

"Did he evict you?" Callum asked in disbelief.

Isabella swallowed the lump that had once again formed in her throat. "No. *She* did. But it's fine. Father left me my dowry, so I have the means to live." She had withdrawn the three hundred pounds with the help of her brother and promptly sewn most of it into the lining of several hats and the hems of two gowns, and hidden some of it in the false bottom of her sewing valise. If she didn't continue to sew for a living, it might last three or four years. Her hope was to find another modiste or two in search of a seamstress.

"But... where?" he asked, in response to her comment about having the means to live.

She lifted a shoulder. "Here," she said. "In Edinburgh. I brought everything I own in a single trunk and a valise on the mail coach."

"So... not much?" he whispered.

She ignored the implication of his simple statement. Her valise contained all the tools of her trade—needles, pins, scissors, a variety of threads, measuring tapes and more. He had probably come to the city with far less, and from what she knew of him from when he still lived in Tideswell—and Daniel obviously agreed —he wasn't one to spend money frivolously. "I have rooms here in New Town," she said, managing to suppress a wince at how much it was costing her. "I think the opportunities are far greater for me here. For employment," she added on a sigh, in case he was imagining another reason for her being there.

Marriage. She would only consider it if it involved an honorable gentleman. Someone with ties to both her childhood home and to Edinburgh.

"Tideswell is rather small," Callum agreed, helping himself to the millefruit biscuit. "When you asked if I might show you where you could find Daniel, was there a particular reason you wished to see him?"

"You mean other than to give my regards to an old friend?" she asked rhetorically.

He cleared his throat. "Fair enough, but what will you do? Here in the city?"

Touched by the concern she heard in his voice, Isabella wondered for a moment why Callum was still unmarried. He was pleasant to look upon, and from what he had said, he was gainfully employed as a clerk. Surely he could afford to take a wife. Then she remembered he was probably too Scotch to marry and decided not to bring up the subject.

"For your living?" he prompted, interrupting her brief reverie.

"Besides being a seamstress?" she replied. She

angled her head to one side and allowed the first sign of humor to appear since she had taken her leave of Daniel's office. If Arthur Peabody had done her bidding—to tell everyone he knew what he had paid witness to after she went into Daniel's office—the resulting gossip might help her secure an advantageous marriage. That she had done far more than she had imagined before going into the office may have only strengthened her standing when it came to the resulting gossip.

Or it could have her branded a brazen hussy. A strumpet. A rake of the female persuasion. She might have to return to Tideswell to escape the gossip.

Besides being a seamstress, what would I do for my living? "I may have already done it," she added, grimacing when she remembered her kiss with Daniel.

His brows furrowing in confusion, Callum watched as she helped herself to the butter biscuit and ate it in three bites.

"Applied for a position, you mean?" he asked.

"Indeed." She lifted her timepiece from where it hung on a chain around her neck and sighed. "I should be getting back to my rooms. If you'll escort me to my building, this will be my treat," she offered, waving to the table. "My rooms aren't far from here."

"Deal," Callum said happily, watching as she fished several coins from her reticule and placed them on the tabletop.

He stood and offered his arm, and the two took their leave of the coffee house to discover the rain had stopped. The sky hadn't cleared, though, the gray clouds suggesting the rain would resume at any moment.

When she directed him to her building, Isabella was sure to mention the number—twice. With any luck, Callum would pass on the information to Daniel when the two next met at a pub for dinner.

CHAPTER 3
NEVER ADMIT
ANYTHING TO A MOTHER

The following afternoon Madeline Sinclair set the tea service on the middle of the parlor's low table and took her regular seat facing the door. "Really, Daniel, must I learn of your improprieties from the neighbor?"

Having left his office early when the continuing rain and dark gray gloom had darkened his office to the point he could no longer work on the McDonald project, Daniel headed for Sinclair House rather than to his favorite pub.

The event from the day before still haunted him—although not necessarily in a bad way. If anyone knew who his caller had been, surely it would be his mother.

Daniel gave a start at hearing her query, though. "Improprieties?" he repeated.

Her quelling glance had him falling into the chair opposite hers.

"Kissing a young lady for just anyone to see?" she said, before lifting the teapot. Hot water splashed over the strainer, and he winced knowing there would be tea leaves aplenty in the bottom of his cup. "I thought I raised you better than to be a... a rake. A rogue," she added with disgust in her voice.

"I didn't kiss her. She kissed me," he argued.

Madeline paused before pouring the next cup. "That's not how the gossip has it happening," she said on a huff.

Remembering she had made reference to the neighbor, Daniel furrowed his dark brows. "I don't understand how anyone can even know of this," he complained. "I was alone in my office—"

"You have a secretary," she reminded him.

Daniel's eyes widened with understanding. "Who is about to become unemployed," he ground out.

"Now, dear, don't be hasty. Mr. Peabody has been a good secretary, and you hardly pay him a living wage," she warned.

"He only has to see to my calendar and copy contracts—"

"Do your correspondence, pay your invoices, and run your errands for you. Act as a courier," she went on. "You must admit he has beautiful penmanship. I should hire him to do my correspondence," she added.

"You're welcome to him," Daniel said, his manner rather grumpy.

Madeline stirred a lump of sugar into her tea. "Who is she?"

Daniel poured a dollop of milk into his tea and sighed. "I was hoping you might know."

His mother straightened in her chair, blinking several times as she regarded him in disbelief. "A woman waltzed into your office—"

"She walked in, Mother. Arthur escorted her," he corrected.

"—and kissed you, and you don't know who she was?"

He cleared his throat. "I... I didn't recognize her," he said, lifting a shoulder. "She obviously knew me, though. Knew Watson, too, because when I accused her of being paid by him—"

"You *what*?" she interrupted.

He immediately regretted his words. "I thought Watson was playing a trick on me. I thought he hired an actress as a sort of prank," he explained.

"Well, that wasn't very smart of you. Everyone knows Watson hasn't a shilling to his name most days," she countered.

"I was reminded of that by the young woman," he murmured. "Which means she knows him," he said thoughtfully. "But I'm still left wondering who she was."

Madeline angled her head to one side. "How old is she?"

He shrugged. "Uh... not a matron. Not fresh out of the schoolroom, either. Mayhap... seven-and-twenty?" he guessed.

"Was she dressed well?"

Daniel winced. "If you can call examples of the current fashion 'dressing well', then yes, I suppose," he hedged. "Big sleeves, bell skirt, jonquil muslin, white shawl... with lace edging," he said, knowing she would press him for the details if he didn't give them up front. "Straw hat, silk flowers on the brim."

She grinned in delight. "You should write for *The Scotsman's* society page," she teased, referring to Edinburgh's weekly newspaper. "As you said, she has obviously met Mr. Watson. What else do you remember about her?"

Frowning, Daniel closed his eyes in an attempt to recall any other details about the woman who had haunted his dreams the night before. The memory of her brought back the new sensations of kissing and his body's reaction to what she had done with her gloved hand.

The tart.

He had been so hard when he awoke in the middle of the night, he had been forced to take his member in hand, shocked that it took only a few seconds for the blessed release that finally allowed him to return to slumber—and more dreams about her.

"Lemons," he murmured. "She smelled of lemons."

Madeline sipped her tea before saying, "Most do these days, dear. It's a popular scent for soaps and such."

"From Derbyshire," he added.

Her eyes widening at hearing this last, his mother grinned. "So... someone you knew from Brookshire Hall," she guessed, referring to her parents' estate. "We spent all our summers there when your father was off on all those building projects," she added.

Daniel nodded. At the time, he had hated what his father did for his living, acting as a contractor for the various canal projects that allowed for goods to be shipped by water rather than by land. The jobs required he be gone for months at a time—the same months Daniel wasn't off at Repton School—but his father had taught him a good deal about construction when he was home. Although Daniel could have easily worked in a building trades, he had opted for the other side of the business—designing the projects.

"A neighbor's daughter, perhaps?"

He shook his head. "Surely I would recognize her," he reasoned. "Not that I recall playing with any girls."

She tittered softly. "Oh, but you did. You attracted them like bees to honey. Still do, I'm quite sure, you handsome beast."

"Mother," he scolded, knowing what she was really thinking. "I'm not going to court anyone, at least, not until I've saved enough to build a house on the outer edge of New Town." He had already designed the villa, a two-story Gothic Revival structure with gardens on three sides and a carriage house and drive on the other. He had purchased the land as soon as he had enough blunt to do so, knowing it would continue to go up in price as Edinburgh expanded northward.

"I know, dear. Now, some girls grow up to appear much prettier than they were in their youth." When he didn't respond right away, she added, "Was she a servant's daughter?"

He pretended to consider it, but thoughts of what it had been like to be kissed had him wishing the woman would make another appearance. Not at his office, though. Somewhere private. Somewhere they wouldn't be seen. The botanic gardens in Inverleith Park, perhaps. Or maybe in one of those tiny squares in Old Town.

Perhaps she would accept his apology for having forgotten her, and he could prove his sincerity by kissing her. Or allowing her to kiss him.

"Did you say *jonquil*?" Madeline asked suddenly.

Pulled from his reverie, Daniel nodded. "Uh, yes. The color of her gown." The color of daffodils and lemons and the sun, if he could ever actually look at it when it was high in the sky.

Madeline's expression of surprise slowly transformed into one of delight. "Oh, Daniel. How could you not recognize Isabella?"

Daniel blinked. And blinked again. "Isabella?" he repeated.

She made a '*tsking*' sound and leaned back in her chair, her face displaying a look of self-satisfaction, as if she had solved the world's greatest mystery. "Isabella Farnsworth. Her father owned the mercantile in Tideswell," she stated, referring to the town nearest Brookshire Hall. "Still does, I think. Her mother..." Here Madeline furrowed her brows and sighed sadly. "Well, it's a wonder Isabella survived childbirth given Mrs. Farnsworth's poor health. It was no surprise she died giving birth to the boy."

His tea forgotten, Daniel stared at his mother. "Was his name Charlie? The boy who always looked as if he'd rolled in the dirt?"

Madeline allowed a wan grin. "As did Isabella. You probably didn't even know she was a girl," she teased. "I'm afraid Mr. Farnsworth wasn't the best at raising his children on his own," she went on. She watched as her son seemed to struggle with his memories. "They were frequently on the grounds of Brookshire Hall when you were there for the summers," she explained. "You used to play in the gardens. Hide and seek. Pall mall when you were older," she continued. "She wore a yellow gown, although it was always filthy, as I recall. You would have thought a father in the mercantile business would have done better at clothing his children, but..." She allowed the sentence to trail off.

"Izzy. She smelled of lemons," Daniel murmured.

Madeline sipped her tea, a lip quirking at seeing her son so perplexed. "And honeysuckle?" she prompted.

Daniel's eyes rounded. "How did you know?"

"The garden was filled with them," she replied.

"They were always full of bees," he whispered.

"The birds would eat the berries," she offered, angling her head as she watched him remember his summers as a youth.

He nodded absently and finally straightened in his chair. "Well, that mystery is solved, I suppose," he said, although his expression suggested he was still vexed.

Madeline leaned forward. "What are you going to do about it?"

He shrugged. "Nothing to do," he responded. When he noticed his mother's look of disappointment, he added, "It's not as if she left a calling card, Mother."

"Are you sure about that?"

Blinking, he settled back in his chair and took a sip of tea as a means to delay his response.

Had the woman given Arthur Peabody her card before she was escorted into the office? If so, Peabody hadn't offered it after she had taken her leave.

"Mayhap she gave a calling card to Peabody," his mother suggested.

The thought that Peabody might know her identity rankled. Daniel was also reminded that only Peabody knew of her visit, which meant he was the one who had been sharing the information as gossip, who knew to how many people?

The fact that his mother's neighbor had been told was probably only a coincidence. Which meant far more people had already heard what had happened in his office, and the gossip was spreading like wildfire.

The details were probably changing with every exchange of the story, too. Her kissing him had probably become him kissing her, which meant his reputation as a perfect gentleman was at risk. His business might even suffer as a result.

Isabella Farnsworth, what have you done? he wondered in dismay.

"You're welcome to stay for dinner," his mother said, interrupting his reverie.

Daniel shook his head. "Thank you for the invitation, but I'm due to meet Watson. We're going to try that new pub on the George the Fourth Bridge."

"Ah, perhaps he'll have some answers for you," she replied.

"Perhaps," he agreed.

CHAPTER 4
A BEST FRIEND CONFESSES

*L*ater *that night, George IV Bar*

Standing at the New Town end of George IV Bridge, Daniel winced at the reminder that two of Old Town's traditional streets, Old Bank Close and Liberton's Wynd, had to be demolished in order to make way for the elevated street that connected New Town to South Side. The George IV Bar was located where the bridge crossed the Cowgate—right in the middle. At the south end was Candlemaker Row.

"Can I afford this?" Callum Watson asked when he joined his friend.

Daniel glanced at the clerk and shrugged. "It's a pub," he replied, before leading them to the new limestone building, it's exterior decorated with columns and corbels. Inside they found a gleaming wood bar lit by hanging lamps and new tables and chairs not yet marred from repeated use.

They both ordered ales and studied the menu board before placing their orders for Scotch pie. Before Daniel could bring up the topic of Isabella Farnsworth, Callum beat him to it.

"I ran into an old friend a couple of days ago," Callum said.

"Oh?" Daniel replied, settling back into his chair, his mug of ale nearly to his lips. He took a sip as Callum nodded and seemed torn as to what he would say next. "Was her name Isabella Farnsworth, by chance?" Daniel asked, leaning forward to place his elbows against the edge of the table.

Callum's eyes rounded. "How did you know?"

Daniel scoffed softly. "She paid a call on me at my office. But you already knew that."

Pretending ignorance, Callum set his mug on the table. "She mentioned she wished to see you again," he hedged.

"Everyone in Edinburgh knows she paid a call," Daniel said on a sigh. "Everyone knows kissing was involved, although I have yet to learn if I am the rake or she is a tart."

"Izzy is not a tart," Callum whispered hoarsely. "How can you say such a thing?"

"She kissed me." Daniel pointed to his cheek. "Here, and then..." He pointed to his lips. "Here. It was... quite *passionate.*" This last was said in a whisper.

"Did you return the kiss?" Callum asked, his manner suggesting he had been waiting for the answer for days and could no longer abide the suspense of not knowing.

Daniel blinked. "Uh, I suppose I did."

"Did you like it?"

"Uh, I suppose I did."

"So... you would do it it again?"

Daniel rolled his eyes. "In private perhaps, but not right out in the open for my secretary—or anyone else —to see."

The two clammed up when the server appeared with their order and set the plates of food in front of them.

"I know where she lives," Callum said before he lifted his fork to stab at the crust covering the Scotch pie.

"Oh, do you?" Daniel countered, deciding he needed to ask Peabody for Isabella's calling card when he was next in the office. He fished in his waistcoat pocket for his small note pad and pencil to make a note of it when the move reminded him of the hole in the side seam.

He had discovered it earlier that morning, immediately reminded of how Isabella's finger had felt when she had been touching him during their kiss. For a brief moment, he had a thought she might have created the tear as a means of ensuring he pay her a call or send a missive about its repair, but then Arthur had made mention of having seen the tear the week before.

Tempted to scold his secretary for not sharing what he had noticed, Daniel had instead decided he could stitch the seam once he was back in his bachelor rooms.

Callum regarded him with surprise. "Have you paid a call on her?"

"Of course not," Daniel said, using his fork to lift the crust from the top of the pie. He set aside the pastry and took a bite of the filling. After he swallowed, he added, "It wouldn't be proper."

"It would be if you were courting her."

Having taken a drink from his mug of ale, Daniel nearly sprayed the liquid over the table. He choked and sputtered before saying, "You of all people know I have every intention of building a house before I even think about courting. Anyone." Although he didn't have any young women in mind for the position of his wife, his brief time with Isabella had awakened something inside him.

The desire for a woman.

He wished he hadn't been so addled by her kiss. If he'd had his wits about him, he would have wrapped his arms around her. Pulled her hard against the front of his body. Felt how her soft curves might fill his voids.

He already knew what it felt like to have her palm pressed against his arousal. His manhood hardened, forcing him to shift in his chair to give it more space at the top of his pantaloons.

Unconsciously, his hand moved to the side seam of his waistcoat, and he poked his finger through the hole. Although he was sure he could see to the repair, he decided he could afford to hire Isabella to do it.

He wanted to hire Isabella.

He wanted to see her again.

She was a reminder of simpler times. Of summers in Derbyshire. Of yellow and sunshine and the scents of lemon and honeysuckle.

He also wanted to scold her for what she had done.

"Her father left her a dowry."

The simple statement brought Daniel out of his brief reverie, and he furrowed his brows. "So that's how she can afford a room in New Town," he murmured, glad she wasn't in one of the crowded buildings in Old Town.

"Well, she is a seamstress," Callum reminded him. "But that's not why I mentioned it."

Daniel took another bite of pie. "Oh? Why then?"

"You wish to build a house. Perhaps her dowry would be enough to pay for it."

Scoffing softly, Daniel considered the suggestion. "I

would have to marry her to gain the dowry," he reasoned.

"You're going to marry her anyway," Callum replied, shrugging before he took another swallow of his ale.

Chuckling softly, Daniel said, "You sound terribly sure of yourself."

"That's because I am."

Although Callum continued to eat his pie, Daniel set his fork on his plate and stared at his friend. "What do you know?"

Callum finished the last bite and used his napkin to dab the corners of his mouth. He leaned back in his chair and folded his arms over his chest. "I've heard the gossip about you. She may have been the one to initiate the kiss, but it's *you* everyone thinks is the rogue."

Daniel sighed in response, wishing there was a way to turn back time. Since it was unlikely he would be able to do that, he pondered hiding for a week or two.

Surely the gossip would die down. It would simply take time, and hopefully not too much of it.

He had a business he wished to keep free from scandal.

CHAPTER 5
A VICTIM OF GOSSIP

he following morning

Opting to take his breakfast at the Tolbooth Tavern, Daniel ducked into the ancient building and inhaled the scents of bacon and freshly baked bread. Located in the Royal Mile in Old Town, the pub offered hearty fare as well as an opportunity to meet with potential clients.

He opted for a small table near the front, the latest copy of *The Scotsman* tucked under his arm. A waiter delivered his usual order only a few minutes later, but before he had a chance to lift his fork, he heard his name and glanced to up to see a middle-aged man in uniform approaching him. "Morning, Colonel Robertson," he said, giving the man a nod.

"Sinclair, so good to see you again. What's this I hear about you and a young lady?" Robertson asked, waggling his bushy brows as he was about to pass by his table.

The officer was in charge of the upkeep of some of the buildings at Edinburgh Castle, and he had hired Daniel in the past to provide his opinion on the fortifications necessary for the older structures. He had been most dismayed by the military's use of St. Margaret's Chapel, the oldest building in all of Scotland, to store gunpowder and other provisions for the personnel barracked at the castle.

"Uh, what have you heard?" Daniel countered, attempting to act as if it was news to him.

"That you kissed her in front of your place of business," Robertson replied, punching Daniel's shoulder. "Right out in the open for anyone to see?" He sighed dramatically. "I had quite forgotten how young love makes a man behave. Been thirty years since I did that with me wife."

Daniel blinked. "I, uh—"

"Courting her, are you?" Robertson interrupted, as if he wished to learn more so he would have first-hand information to share with his garrison.

Dipping his head, Daniel realized two things at the same time. If he denied courting the girl, his kiss would be seen as the socially unacceptable behavior of a rake. His business would no doubt suffer. Who would wish to hire an architect with a reputation as a rogue?

However, if he agreed, at least he would have an acceptable excuse for having participated in the kiss.

"You've sorted it perfectly, Colonel," he replied, glad for the darkened interior that hid his reddening face. "Have you any other buildings requiring my expert evaluation?" he added, hoping to steer the conversation to work. "I'm drafting a house on a commission now, but I should have some time in a few weeks."

"Not yet, but perhaps next year," Robertson replied. "Why, you'll probably be a married man by then," he said happily. "Best wishes."

"Uh, if she says 'yes'," Daniel hedged, relieved he remembered he had an easy out should the topic come up again.

"No young lady would be fool enough to turn down marriage to a handsome bloke like you," Robertson said, chuckling as he took his leave of the tavern.

Daniel watched the man leave before returning his attention to his breakfast. The plate of poached eggs, smoked fish, and brown bread still appeared edible, but the syrup atop his bowl of porridge had cooled, as had his coffee.

Before he finished eating, two more gentlemen had stopped by his table with their greetings. At least neither brought up the errant kiss, but he heard the unmistakeable sound of lips smacking as they departed.

*A*n hour later

Striding into the building in which his office was located, its white limestone blocks washed clean from the incessant rain of the past two days, Daniel shed his great coat and approached his secretary's desk.

"Morning, Peabody. Any correspondence?" he asked, tamping down the desire to scold the man for the gossip he had obviously started. He secretly wanted to terminate the man's employment, but his mother's words reminded him he wouldn't be able to find a suitable replacement with the same skills for the same pay.

Given the teasing he had suffered at the tavern and remembering what his mother had said, he knew the secretary had shared news of his kiss with Isabella Farnsworth. The betrayal rankled.

"When she was here the other day, did Miss Farnsworth leave you a calling card?" he asked, as Peabody took his coat.

His secretary's eyes widened slightly even as a flush of red crept up and colored his high cheekbones. "She did, sir," he admitted. He hung the greatcoat on a peg on the wall and returned to his desk. Although the papers on it were neatly stacked, he seemed to have trouble locating the pasteboard card. When he finally held it out to his employer, he asked, "Is she a potential client, sir?" his query made in an innocent-sounding voice.

Daniel gave him a withering glance. "She had better be," he grumbled, thinking of the house he had designed and wanted to build before taking a wife. He didn't bother to read the card until he was in his office and the door was closed.

Centered in black ink on the front were the words:

Miss Isabella Farnsworth

Seamstress

and on the back:

~For an appointment, send inquiries to~

The space below had been left blank by the printer, but an address was handwritten in a feminine script.

Hurrying over to one of the walls without a window, Daniel studied the large map of Edinburgh he had purchased the year before. He had filled in several open spaces with new projects that had been built since its publication and marked others with an 'X' if he knew they were to be demolished. Finally locating the approximate location of the address he found on the card, he gave a start.

New Town, he confirmed. Just as Callum had said the night before. How could his friend from childhood afford such an address, though? Was this her place of business? Or where she lived? Or both?

Well, she is a seamstress, he remembered. *And she has her dowry.*

Daniel pulled out his timepiece and glanced back at his drafting table. Given the sky was fairly clear, the light was bright enough to work without burning several candle lamps. In a few hours, the sun would no longer be at the right angle to illuminate his workspace.

Torn between tracking down Isabella or seeing to his current project, he opted to remain in the office.

He discovered he had made the right choice not long after.

CHAPTER 6
A JUDGE'S DECREE

*I*n the office of D. Sinclair, Architect

Taking his seat at his drafting table, Daniel immediately resumed his work on the McDonald house, thoughts of where to place the parlor and the library in the first floor apparently conjuring the client himself into existence.

"Mr. Sinclair, Lord McDonald is here to see you," Arthur said from the door.

Daniel glanced up, shocked to discover he had been so consumed with the project, he hadn't noticed his client's arrival nor the passage of nearly two hours of time.

"Lord McDonald! Do come in," he said, stepping off his stool to greet one of the Senators of the College of Justice, a judge at Scotland's supreme civil court.

The two shook hands as Geoffrey McDonald

glanced around the small office. "Sinclair. I have to admit, I'm a bit surprised to find you all alone in here," the judge said, a teasing grin appearing to lift the man's round cheeks.

"My lord?" Daniel replied, displaying a quizzical expression.

McDonald crossed his arms over his paunch and chuckled. "Well, this *is* where the infamous kiss took place, is it not?"

Daniel blinked. "Uh, oh. That." He waved a hand dismissively. "I'm afraid a peck on the cheek from an old friend has been taken quite of context, my lord," he explained.

His face falling, McDonald's arms dropped to his sides. "What's this?"

"I'm not sure what you've heard—"

"That you and a rather attractive young lady in a yellow gown—"

"Jonquil," he interrupted, immediately wincing at having essentially admitted his part in the event. "She was wearing a jonquil gown," he murmured.

The correction on the color barely slowed down McDonald, though. "You and an attractive young lady in a *jonquil* gown were seen in a rather passionate embrace, kissing as if she had accepted your offer of marriage."

Daniel blinked again. *Offer of marriage?* "I wouldn't call it a 'passionate embrace', my lord." Realizing the judge wasn't about to accept his clarification, Daniel struggled to sort what to say before McDonald once again crossed his arms.

"Tell me there is a wedding in your future, son."

"There is a wedding in my future," Daniel repeated, deciding he wasn't exactly lying. *The distant future.* He had every intention of taking a wife once he had finished building his house. After he had saved enough blunt to do so.

"Good. If you decide on a civil ceremony over one in the church, I certainly know where that can be arranged," McDonald said, his glee returning as he waggled his brows. "Who is she?"

Daniel took a steadying breath. "Miss Isabella Farnsworth. I, uh, knew her... uh, *know* her from where I spent my summers growing up in Derbyshire."

Angling his balding head to one side, the judge seemed ever so pleased. "Derbyshire? So she's English?" Usually the word would be accompanied by a look of derision, but in this case the judge didn't seem particularly offended.

"She is, my lord," Daniel acknowledged.

"Good family?"

Lifting a shoulder, Daniel remembered what his mother had told him. "Her father owned the mercantile in Tideswell, but now that he's expired, her brother runs it," he explained.

"Ah, so her brother has been seeing to her welfare then?"

Daniel once again blinked. "She has been seeing to herself since her brother recently married," he said, arching a brow to show his displeasure with the man. What brother would allow his wife to kick his sister out of the house? "She recently moved to Edinburgh, I suppose so she could gain more clients. She is a seamstress by trade, you see, and Tideswell is rather small," he added, hoping he had the details right. Everything he knew about Isabella he had learned second-hand.

"All the more reason you should see to marrying her sooner rather than later."

Daniel swallowed, glad his cravat hid his reaction. "Of course, my lord."

"My wife is going to demand a new ballgown for the Peers' Ball next week. Do you suppose Miss Farnsworth would be able to fit it into her schedule?"

"Uh... I could ask her to pay a call on Lady McDonald, if you'd like," Daniel offered, not sure he should simply answer in the affirmative. In an effort to change the subject, he glanced over at the drafting table, the large surface angled in the opposite direction so the house plans couldn't be seen from where they stood. "If you've the time, I wondered if I might ask your opinion as to the placement of the parlor and library in your new house?"

The judge arched a brow. "I'll take a look, but I may

have to send Lady McDonald for her opinion," he hedged, making his way to the other side of the table. His bushy brows rose in appreciation. "You're nearly finished," he said in awe, noting the stack of elevations at the top of the table and the first floor spread out on the smooth wood surface. Metal clips at the edges of the table held the vellum in place.

"I still have the second and third floors to do, although I do have them sketched out," Daniel said. "To be certain the windows line up evenly."

"Symmetry is important," McDonald commented, pulling out a pair of spectacles. He set them on the edge of his nose

"But the ground floor is ready," Daniel continued. "I did as you asked and put the study down there." He pulled out another huge sheet of vellum—the ground floor plan—and settled it over the top of the first floor drawing. "There's still space for a sitting room or a small parlor, and you'll have a music room here—" he pointed to a room on the right side, "—and the ballroom here with a wall of windows looking out on a garden," he said as he pointed to the left side of the layout. "Cloak room, retiring rooms," he added, waving to an area near the ballroom but closer to the round entrance.

"I like how you have the stairs curving up to the first floor. My wife will reward me when she sees those," he said, his brows waggling. "Should they be made of marble, do you suppose?"

"They would be magnificent in marble, my lord," Daniel replied, relieved the judge wasn't deterred by such a costly feature. "As would the floor. The curve is repeated in the wall on left of the entry," he explained, pulling the drawing of the front elevation from the stack and lining it up over the floor plan. "Which goes all the way up to the roof, as does the curved wall on the right, so the front of the house will appear as a half-cylinder with columns on either side and a set of double doors in the center."

McDonald examined the elevation drawing and nodded appreciatively. He returned his attention to the first floor plan. "Parlor should be right at the top of the stairs, and..." He used a pudgy finger and pointed to where Daniel had penciled in the word 'library' in the space next to the parlor with a question mark. "Let's put the library downstairs next to the study."

"Downstairs?" Daniel repeated in surprise.

"The fewer stairs I have to climb, the better," the judge commented. "In fact, just put the study *in* the library..." He pointed to the area where Daniel had indicated a small parlor could be located. "And then you can double the size of the parlor on the first floor. Clara will be able to host her hen parties in a single room rather than having to flit about several rooms in an effort to make everyone feel welcome."

Daniel suppressed the urge to grin, his imagination conjuring Lady McDonald hurrying from one room to the next, never having the chance to actually sit and play cards or drink tea—or whatever it was that ladies drank at hen parties.

A larger parlor meant there wouldn't be a support wall, though. He quickly decided where he could place a row of support columns, their capitals carved in the manner of the Greek Doric style. "Very well, my lord. Is there anything else you'd like me to include?"

The judge considered his query a moment and sighed. "I suppose I should be sure the second floor has those newfangled bathing chambers next to the bedchambers," he said.

"I'll be sure they're included," Daniel replied. "I, uh, I have included one off the parlor," he added, pointing to a small room at the back. "And one down here near your study." He lifted the vellum to point to a small room directly beneath the one he had referenced at the back of the parlor.

"Capital," McDonald replied. "Make the one off the parlor a bit larger, would you? These lady's gowns aren't getting any smaller, dammit. The only ones benefitting from those huge skirts are the drapers and textile manufacturers," he groused.

Daniel grinned. "My sentiments exactly," he agreed. "I shall see to enlarging the retiring rooms," he added, writing a few quick notes in the margins of the floor plan. When he glanced up, he discovered the judge watching him, a pained expression on his face. "What is it, my lord?"

McDonald shook his head. "For a man who looks as if Aphrodite and Apollo were his parents, you're not particularly vain, are you?"

Opening his mouth to respond, Daniel quickly closed it but chuckled. He finally lifted a shoulder in a shrug of resignation. "I can't really help how I look, sir," he said.

"You could be an exhibit in your own zoo and be charging admission. Then you'd have enough blunt to marry in only a week or two."

Daniel's face flushed red. "Thank you. I think," he replied.

"The sooner you're off the marriage mart, the better it will be for the rest of us mortal men."

Dipping his head, Daniel murmured, "I have every intention of marrying, once I can afford a wife."

"Well, send me an invoice for what you've done so far," McDonald ordered, waving to the floor plans. "That should be enough to tide you over until they're all done. I'll sign the contract your secretary sent and be sure to send other potential clients your way."

Daniel swallowed at hearing the judge's comment. "Yes, my lord. Thank you."

With that, Lord Geoffrey McDonald took his leave of Daniel's office.

When Daniel noticed Arthur's attention directed at him, he cocked a dark brow.

The secretary bowed to the judge and waited until the man was out the door before he joined Daniel in his office.

"What is it?" Daniel asked.

"This arrived for you whilst you were with his lordship," Arthur said, holding out a white envelope.

Daniel furrowed a brow, taking the missive in hand. "Who delivered it?" he asked, studying the writing which included only his name in an even script on the front.

"A caddy. Not one I recognized," Arthur replied, referring to the young boys who acted as couriers in the city.

Daniel unfolded the envelope and frowned as he read the feminine script.

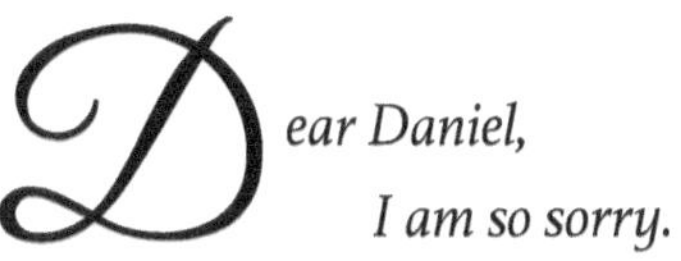

ear Daniel,

I am so sorry.

I never intended for our brief reunion to result in yours —or my—ruination. I was so overcome by the sight of you —how is it a man can be so handsome as you are?—I could not help my reaction.

Can you ever forgive me? I'll do whatever I must to correct this most unfortunate situation.

With my sincerest apologies,

Isabella

aniel furrowed his brows as he reread the missive, a multitude of emotions clashing until he didn't know what he should think or how he would respond.

He had a thought to be vindictive. Force her to marry him on the morrow—Lord McDonald had intimated he could see to an expedited civil ceremony— but he quickly set aside the idea. He wasn't sure he could afford a wife, even if he economized—and even if McDonald paid his invoice as quickly as he suggested he might.

Where would they live?

He had a thought to simply ignore the missive. Pretend he hadn't read it. Act as if it had never been delivered. *Ignorance is bliss.*

Except it wasn't.

How could it be when he realized how his body was reacting to the idea of marriage to *her*. He couldn't recall a single time since his later years in school that he experienced such a visceral reaction to just the thought of a woman.

His last thought was to simply acknowledge her apology in the manner it was intended. She had been overcome. She was sorry.

I'll do whatever I must to correct this most unfortunate situation.

For a moment after reading the words 'unfortunate situation', he felt a hint of disappointment.

If she saw it as an 'unfortunate situation', did that mean she regretted kissing him? For a reason other than the gossip that had everyone thinking him a rake?

Had his kiss been that bad?

It wasn't as if he'd had any experience in the matter. Kissing was an intimate act. More so than sexual congress. His recollection of their kiss had him thinking it a rather pleasant experience. He would have liked a bit more... notice. A bit of warning, so he could have prepared. So he could have angled his head in the correct position. So he would have known where to place his hands.

Although, until he had actually experienced it, he wouldn't have known such things.

Without realizing it, he was pantomiming the very actions he was imagining. He was also unaware Arthur was regarding him with an expression of confusion. When his secretary cleared his throat, Daniel immediately straightened and sounded a curse.

"Did you wish to send a reply, sir?" Arthur asked.

Daniel shook his head. "I think I should answer this in person," he murmured. He glanced back at his drafting table, deciding the best light of the day had already passed. A candle lamp or two would be required for him to continue his work this afternoon.

Perhaps it wouldn't rain on the morrow.

"I'll need my topcoat," he said as he refolded the missive and stuffed it into his waistcoat pocket.

Arthur nodded and moved to pull the garment from the peg near his desk. "Should I hail a hackney for you, sir?"

Daniel shook his head as he unrolled his shirt sleeves and secured the buttons at the cuffs. "I'll walk," he replied, donning both his topcoat and his greatcoat. He pulled on his gloves and said, "His lordship said he will sign the contract you sent. You're to bill him for the work I've done so far on his house plans. See to an invoice, will you? Four elevations, one ground floor plan."

"Yes, sir."

"If I'm not back by six o'clock, lock up the office and take your leave."

*N*odding, Arthur rushed back to his desk. He watched as his employer exited the office, a look of uncertainty crossing his face.

Either he had made a huge mistake in following the instructions of the young lady who had paid a call earlier that week—and he would lose his position as a result—or he had assisted in seeing to it his employer married sooner rather than later.

At least the judge was on his side.

CHAPTER 7
DISCUSSING A PROPOSITION

a half-hour later

Ensconced in the chair nearest a window, Isabella completed the last small stitches in a seam before knotting the thread. When she shook out the garment, she stood and held it up in front of her body.

She wished there was a looking glass large enough to reflect the entirety of the sapphire silk ballgown. Madame Laurent's design was exquisite, the choice of fabric perfect for an aristocratic lady. Both puffy sleeves were finished, their gathers evenly spaced where they met the long cuffs, and were ready to be sewn onto the gown's armholes. If the light held, she might finish it this afternoon.

She was about to pin the sleeves to the gown when a knock at the door had her giving a start. Before she had a thought she should hang the gown on a peg, she hurried to the door. She used her slippered foot to coax a rolled rug into place a few inches from the bottom of the wood panel. Should whoever was on the other side attempt to force it open, the rug would prevent the door from swinging open more than a few inches.

Opening the door until it hit the rug, she peeked out the thin opening. She blinked and inhaled sharply.

Isabella wasn't sure why her first thought was to shut the door.

Daniel Sinclair was here. In her building. At her door. Looking every bit as handsome and—dare she think it?—kissable—as the day she had interrupted his work and kissed him.

"Hello, Daniel." She sighed, immediately understanding why he was there. "You must have received my note of apology."

Before she could think of what else to say, Daniel nervously glanced both left and right before saying, "I did. Either you must come out here, or you must invite me in there." His words were said in a quiet voice. "We need to talk."

Recovering from her moment of shock, Isabella stepped back and remembered too late she still held the ball gown in front of her body.

"That's a rather gorgeous gown," he whispered, ducking his head from side to side so he could see all of it despite the small opening.

"Thank you. I made it," she said, before hanging it on a nearby peg. "Well, most of it. The pieces were already cut out. I've just had to stitch it together."

"Is it for you? Or—?"

"A client," she replied, wondering at the awe she heard in his voice. "A judge's wife. One of the modistes here in town has hired me to sew for her," she added, grabbing her shawl and reticule from another peg next to the door. "Although I'm not afraid of you coming in —for myself or for my reputation—I fear for yours should anyone see you," she said, pushing the rolled rug out of the way so she could open the door wider. She stepped out and turned around to lock the door, a metal key held in one hand.

"It's a bit too late for that," he said, offering his arm when she was beside him.

She glanced up, her eyes rounding. "Oh, dear. What's happened?"

Of course she hadn't considered the ramifications of being seen kissing him at his place of business, because truth be told, she hadn't intended to kiss him on the lips.

She had thought to only kiss him on the cheek. A kiss of friendship, much like how the French greeted one another.

Instructing his secretary to share the news of what he was about to witness ensured others would learn of it, but she hadn't planned to kiss Daniel the way she had. It had just... *happened*. She had merely wished others to learn of her call on him. Some would assume she was securing his services as an architect while others would think there was more to it and probably tease Daniel. Prod him a bit. Encourage him to consider marriage.

It wasn't supposed to lead to widespread gossip or a stain on his good name.

Daniel led her down the corridor to the stairs. "I seem to have acquired a reputation as a rake," he said. "Through no fault of my own."

Isabella didn't bother hiding her look of guilt. "I'm so sorry. I... I couldn't help myself," she claimed.

"Oh?" He seemed surprised by her comment as he opened the outer door to the building.

"Have you looked at yourself in a mirror?" she asked playfully.

He scoffed and rolled his eyes. "I cannot help how I appear to others," he claimed, annoyance sounding in his voice.

Undaunted by his poor mood, Isabella displayed a grin of delight. "I don't know how the ladies here in Edinburgh are able to control themselves around you," she said. "Unless they're blind. I see you, and all I want to do is throw myself into your arms and kiss you senseless." She blinked and turned to find him staring down at her with an expression of disbelief.

Then he suddenly barked a laugh. "Really, Izzy. I

assure you, every woman I have come across has been able to..." Here he stopped, remembering what Lord McDonald had said only the hour before in his office. Remembering all the times he had noticed women staring at him. Gawking at him. Waving their fans in front of their faces as if they were suddenly rather warm. "Well, that is, none of *them* have kissed me," he finished.

"But they *wanted* to," she countered, directing a teasing grin at him. She could feel the heat of a blush on her cheeks, stunned at how forward she was being with him. But what had she to lose? She had already kissed him. Already admitted she wanted to do it again.

"If you say so," he murmured, his hurried steps forcing her to nearly run to keep up.

"Where are we going?" she asked.

"Somewhere private," he replied curtly, although he slowed his pace. After a short pause, he added, "Callum said your father has died."

"Yes," she responded, nearly breathless from struggling to keep up.

"Charlie has the mercantile now?"

"Yes, and he has married a woman from Buxton. She didn't want me living with them, so I had to leave." She watched as his expression softened, as if he had been annoyed with her but was no longer.

"So you moved *here* of all places?"

"I did. I wished to live in a city where I knew someone—"

"Me?" he interrupted, his gaze on her one of surprise.

"And Callum. I've an ancient great aunt near here, too, but I'm not sure exactly where she lives." She paused before adding, "This is a city where I can make my living as a seamstress and..." She let the sentence trail off.

"And?" he prompted.

"In Scotland, I don't require a man to see to my money."

Daniel suddenly slowed his steps even more. "Your dowry?" he guessed.

She nodded, her eyes widening when she noted how his expression had changed again. His entire manner had, in fact, changed. "What is it?"

He didn't answer immediately, instead leading her across the street and into a park. Crushed limestone crunched beneath their feet as they followed the path between leafy sycamores and cherry trees that had shed their spring blooms. The late afternoon sun had already painted the western sky in shades of peach and apricot, and a slight breeze rustled the leaves. "I have a proposition for you," he said suddenly.

"A proposition?" she repeated, thinking the term rather odd.

"Indeed. Hear me out, and afterwards I'd like to

learn what you think of it," he said, his brows furrowing so he appeared far older than his seven-and-twenty years.

Isabella nodded. "All right."

He took a deep breath and let it out. "I had a plan," he stated. "If you had asked me last week what it was, I would have told you I needed to secure more clients so I could afford to build a house. I already have the land, you see,—"

"Oh, where?" she asked with excitement.

"Uh, over there," he said, pointing to an area on the northern edge of New Town. "You can't see the exact lot from here, but it's in that general direction."

"You have it all designed, I suppose?" she asked, her gaze entirely on him. She trusted him enough to know he wouldn't have them walking into a tree or a lamp post.

"I do. I thought to build it, and then, after a few more projects—a few years later—I would be able to afford to take a wife."

She inhaled softly. "Do you have someone in mind? To be your wife?"

"I don't... I... I didn't," he stammered. "It's always been a house first, then a wife. That was the plan."

When he didn't say anything more, she said, "It sounds as if you haven't taken the benefits of a dowry into consideration."

For a moment, Daniel looked as if he was suffering

from indigestion. He dipped his head. "A dowry is supposed to be used for a woman's future, especially if there are children," he argued. "For when her husband dies, so she has the means to carry on," he added.

Isabella's eyes rounded. "Really?"

"What did you think it was for?"

She lifted a shoulder. "To pay off gambling debts?"

Daniel barked a laugh. "I suppose there are situations where that might be the case," he hedged.

"But you're not a gambler?" she guessed.

He shook his head. "I play cards on occasion, but not for money," he admitted.

She nodded, secretly glad he wasn't in debt. "How much do you need? To build the house?" She prepared herself to hear an astronomical number, sure there were houses in Edinburgh that cost upwards of two-thousand pounds. She had seen the sales sheets in the windows of agents, read the postings in *The Scotsman* of estates for sale.

He winced. "Two-hundred... two-hundred-and-thirty pounds," he replied.

She gasped. "I have it," she said with excitement.

Giving a start, Daniel furrowed his brows. "You have two-hundred-and thirty pounds?" he asked, obviously surprised.

"More than that," she said.

Daniel stared at her in disbelief, his expression slowly changing until he seemed humbled by her claim. "I don't wish to be in debt to you, Izzy," he said. "But I do appreciate the offer. If... if that's what it was?" The look of uncertainty on his face suggested he was at war with himself.

Isabella couldn't help the disappointment she felt. "I only mentioned my dowry because, well, it will go to whomever I marry."

Daniel inhaled sharply. "Are you betrothed to someone?"

She shook her head. "Not yet. You mentioned a proposition," she reminded him.

He nodded and displayed another wince. "I did, but now it seems terribly... unfair," he murmured.

"Unfair how?" she countered.

Leading them to a park bench, he used his handkerchief to brush off the wood slats and waited for her to sit before he took the seat next to her. "Do you wish to be married?" he asked.

She grinned. "I do, but only if I feel affection for the gentleman."

Daniel made an odd sound in his throat. "You kissed me, Izzy."

"I did," she acknowledged, grinning as if the memory made her happy.

He nodded slowly, although his brows showed his worry. "Have you kissed anyone else?"

"Of course not." When he still seemed uncertain, she asked, "What is it, Danny?"

. . .

The name Daniel had answered to as a child had him straightening on the bench, memories from their youth reminding him of how happy he had been when Isabella was nearby. How they had played in the gardens of Brookshire Hall. How her blonde hair blew in the breeze as they ran over the clipped lawn in their bare feet.

He had a thought of how she might look now if her hair wasn't caught up in a bun and partially covered by a hat. What it would feel like splayed over his bare chest after they made love.

Another part of him was already anticipating such a union. He shifted on the bench in an effort to make room for it.

"You do realize that if I were to propose matrimony right here and now, you will never know if I did so to simply silence the gossips or because I wished for your dowry or because... because I feel affection for you," he murmured.

"Promise to marry me, and you can discover the answer tonight," she whispered.

"Izzy," he breathed, wondering if she knew her answer didn't match the question.

Or perhaps it did.

"You're sure you want this?"

She nodded. "I would not have come to Edinburgh if I didn't."

He narrowed his eyes. "So you *did* move here because of me?"

Dipping her head, she took a breath and sighed. "I did so miss seeing your handsome face," she admitted.

Chuckling softly, Daniel took her gloved hand in his and rested it on his thigh. At no point did she attempt to prevent him from doing so, nor did she seem particularly bothered by the move. In fact, her eyes seemed to sparkle with mischief, much as they had when they were younger. He recognized her then.

Isabella Farnsworth. The perfect playmate on days both sunny and cloudy. Armed with a mallet, she could whack the wooden ball through a series of wickets in every game of pall mall. She frequently lost at hide and seek, usually because her yellow frock made it impossible for her to stay hidden in the garden. As for archery, he recalled it was far better to remain well behind her or risk being shot with an arrow.

Perhaps Cupid had been controlling her aim even back then.

"You are the female equivalent of a rogue, aren't you?" he teased, the oddest sensation gripping his chest.

She displayed a wan grin. "Until you make an honest woman of me, I suppose I am."

He narrowed his eyes, realizing that unless they married—and quickly—gossip would paint her as his mistress, or worse, a strumpet. The need to protect her suddenly consumed him.

"So... you'll marry me?" he asked, nearly wincing at how desperate he sounded.

She blinked, apparently not expecting the query. "Is... is that a proposal?"

Although Daniel Sinclair hadn't spent much time considering how he would acquire a wife, he had never thought it would be as simple as this. Someone with whom he had enjoyed spending time in his youth was offering herself—and a dowry—to be his wife.

He would be a fool not to take advantage of the situation.

But was it fair to her? What would be in it for her?

A gainfully employed friend who happened to be handsome.

Isabella seemed terribly willing. She had already admitted her move to Edinburgh was due to him. "Yes," he said in answer to her proposal question. He glanced around where they sat, finally locating a small dandelion bloom. Much as they had done when they were younger, he plucked it from the grass and quickly formed it into a ring by tying the end of the stem near the yellow flower.

"What are you doing?" she asked in fascination.

"Making you a betrothal ring. This will have to do

until I can retrieve my grandmother's ring from Sinclair House and line up a wedding date with Lord McDonald." When he saw her eyes widening, he added, "He's a judge in the civil court. Said he could see to a quick ceremony for us."

"Oh, did he now?" she said, displaying a look of awe. She removed her glove so he could slide the dandelion onto her finger.

"Indeed. Seems my reputation has been questioned, and I'm determined to set my best client straight on the matter. Plus he intends to pay for the work I've completed on his house plans."

She wiggled her fingers and grinned. "I do like yellow."

"As do I," he said.

The two stared at one another for a few seconds before they leaned in for a kiss at the very same time. Having a moment to prepare, Daniel knew exactly where to place his hands, exactly how to angle his head so he could simply enjoy the intimate exchange.

They might have continued the kiss for far longer than they did but for the sound of disgust emanating from a female passerby.

"She said yes!" Daniel called out, hoping to excuse his behavior with the matron.

"You're a cabbage-headed fool," came the response.

Daniel scoffed as Isabella giggled in delight. When she finally sobered, she said, "Let's have dinner at a pub. You can tell me all about your life since you moved here, and then you can take me to my rooms."

He nodded. "And after that?"

She grinned again. "I'm going to discover if you feel affection for me."

Momentarily shocked by the comment, Daniel barked a laugh. "Oh, I do love a challenge," he murmured. He stood and offered a hand, and the two took their leave of the park.

CHAPTER 8
A LUSTY AFFECTION

few hours later

As Isabella lounged against the iron headboard of her bed, a pillow protecting her bare back from the rails and one knee bent to act as a work surface, she made the last few stitches necessary to repair the side seam of Daniel's waistcoat.

Knotting the thread, she carefully clipped it with the tiny scissors she had retrieved from the nightstand and then shook out the garment.

Holding it by the shoulders, she pulled it to her face and inhaled deeply, the scents of musk and citrus reminding her of the day she had entered Daniel's office and kissed him. If it hadn't been for the tear in the seam, her finger would never have been caught, and she might not have discovered his ardor for her.

The owner of said waistcoat was sound asleep

farther down the bed, his face pressed against a thigh, a heavy arm draped over her leg. She had already seen to pulling the bed linens over most of his body. Although she enjoyed studying his nakedness—he was as beautiful in body as his face was handsome—it was a distraction she couldn't afford when she was sewing.

Twice she had pricked her thumb with the needle before realizing she simply had to cover his backside.

Although he had warned her he might take a short nap after their bout of playful lovemaking, she hadn't expected him to be out as long as he had been.

How could a man sleep after lovemaking? Isabella's entire body buzzed with excitement. Every nerve ending seemed especially sensitive. Warmth permeated her extremities, making it easy to sew.

Upon their return from the pub, they had stood in front of the fireplace and merely stared at each other. Their undressing of one another had begun slowly, carefully, as if they both feared tearing the other's clothes.

Once Daniel had her gown, petticoats, and corset off of her, his questing hands had explored every inch of her, as if he were a blind man studying a statue.

She hadn't remained inert, though, her own hands making quick work of the buttons of his top coat and waistcoat, the fastenings of his pantaloons, and the knot of his cravat. Slowly unwrapping the length of silk from around his neck, she tittered when he attempted to rid himself of his shirt before she had it completely removed. Despite his protestations, she had taken great care to fold the cravat and shirt and drape them over the back of a chair.

By the time she was back in his hold, wearing only her shift and stockings, he had stripped his pantaloons and stockings from his body. His manhood, fully erect, jutted from its nest of curls and bobbed about in anticipation of what was about to happen.

Curiosity had her gingerly touching it, first with a forefinger. When he guided her hand to wrap it around the velvety soft skin, she delighted in how it throbbed in her hold, how he inhaled sharply when she used the fingers of her other hand to explore his ball sac, lifting it until he abruptly growled and stepped back.

Meanwhile, she had been entirely unaware of how he had plucked every pin from her hair, the blonde locks cascading down in waves around her face as she played with his engorged member.

"Now you've done it," he whispered hoarsely, although his grin belied the sound of warning in his voice.

For a moment, she wondered what he had done with the hairpins. Then she watched as he reached for the mantel. She heard the metallic clinking sounds as he opened his fist and they fell from his grasp.

Whatever modesty she might have possessed took its leave when next he stripped her of her shift, revealing a pair of breasts with nipples already pinched and aching to be suckled. Apparently he understood, for once he had his arms wrapped around her shoulders, his mouth was on them, licking and nibbling while he groaned and she gasped at the frissons darting about beneath her skin. When her fingers speared his dark hair, she scraped his scalp with her nails and giggled when his entire body shivered.

A moment later, and she was on her bed, her knees bent and spread wide as he used his fingers to coax her to a most wondrous sensation. When he replaced his fingers with the tip of his manhood, she heard his moan and watched as his face took on an expression of bliss.

How could an already handsome man appear even more so?

Apparently whatever she did next was the right thing to do, for he was suddenly filling her near to bursting, his murmured 'yes's' and 'oh my god's' sounding as if they were said as prayers. A moment or two of repeated retreats and thrusting, and he suddenly stilled, raised his head, and said, "Oh, Isabella."

Perhaps he was worshipping her, the bed a sort of altar. If so, she hoped he might do so more often than once a week.

"You have thoroughly ruined me, you rogue," she remembered murmuring when he settled his head next to hers, the sound of her subsequent titter at odds with reality.

"It takes one to know one, you minx," he had whispered, right before he passed out.

*A*fter setting aside the waistcoat, Isabella attempted to shift her body down the bed without disturbing Daniel. He awoke, though, his brows furrowing when he saw where she had been lying.

"How can you still be awake?" he asked, his voice thick with slumber.

"I was too excited to sleep," she whispered. "This is the first time I've ever had a rogue in my bed."

"You had best get used to it," he murmured. "I intend to be here every night," he added, yawning. "That is, until our bedchamber is finished in the house." His attention went beyond her to the nightstand. "Is that my waistcoat?"

She nodded. "I repaired it," she said, showing him where she had stitched the hole in the side seam. There was no sign it had ever been damaged.

"Thank you," he whispered, kissing her arm. "Will you sleep with me now?" he asked, using an arm to pull her body down until she was tucked up against his. "We have a big day tomorrow," he added, cradling her hand in his, its dandelion ring still adorning the fourth finger.

"You say that as if we're getting married," she teased.

"That's my intention," he replied. When she turned her head back to glance at him in surprise, he added, "Remember, I have clients in high places."

"As do I," she replied. She felt him suddenly stiffen and realized he had misunderstood her comment. "The ballgown I am making is for Lady McDonald, the judge's wife. The Peer's Ball is next week."

Although Daniel felt a good deal of relief at hearing the words, he also felt pride on her behalf. "Something tells me the *on-dit* about us will be quite different in a day or so," he murmured happily.

Isabella sighed contentedly. "I think we both know someone who can see to it that it does," she whispered. She didn't have to mention his secretary by name.

CHAPTER 9
EPILOGUE

A year later, on the north side of New Town

Barely able to contain her excitement, Isabella bounced on the balls of her feet as she held her hands over her eyes. "Can I look now?" she asked, glad Daniel still had his hands on her arms to guide her. She was sure her slippered feet were on a clipped lawn while the unmistakeable sounds of pounding and sawing could be heard in the distance.

Another new house was going up somewhere nearby.

"You can look," he said, his voice coming from in front of her.

She opened her eyes, blinking at the sudden brightness. Directly in front of her, Daniel stood watching her as he smiled.

Isabella giggled in delight. "Oh, Daniel, you're so handsome when you grin like that," she said, pretending to ignore the structure behind him.

Daniel sobered and scoffed. "You're supposed to be looking at the *house*," he said, stepping aside to give her an unimpeded view of their Gothic Revival house, the two-story structure built with blocks of limestone cemented with harling.

A single turret with windows, its conical roof tiled in slate, stood at one front corner of the house while the rest of the asymmetrical design featured two gables, their roofs also topped in slate. A pair of Palladian windows framed the arched set of double doors on the ground floor, and above those, the second story featured four rectangular windows.

"It's gorgeous. It's just like your drawings," she said, taking a few steps forward. She paused and glanced down at the lawn. "Is this our grass?"

Chuckling, he took her hand in his. "It is."

"It's so green," she said, her gaze going from the lawn to the house. No ornamental bushes adorned the front of the house, but she knew some would be added soon.

"Let me show you inside. The colorman is seeing to the nursery, so its yet to be painted," he warned, his gaze darting to where her yellow gown did little to hide her advanced pregnancy.

"What color will it be?"

"Jonquil, of course," he replied. He opened the front door and allowed her to step inside the hall before he joined her.

She gasped, her gaze immediately going to the ornate plaster ceiling and then to the stone fireplace set in a wall made entirely of stone. The floors, wood planks sanded smooth, had been stained and varnished. A set of spiral stone stairs occupied the turret.

"We'll have gas heating in the winters, and there's a water closet upstairs," he said proudly. "With a shower."

"We could afford that?" she asked in surprise.

He nodded. "I did some work in trade," he explained. "A set of plans for the man who did the pipes for both and did all the necessary plumbing." He pulled her farther into the front hall, the arched doorway directly ahead leading into a dining room.

"We have a chandelier," Isabella said in awe. Although there weren't yet any furnishings in the house, she could imagine how the table they had ordered would fit, how a sideboard could be placed at one end.

"A bit of a splurge, but I thought it worth it," he said. "After hearing Lord McDonald sing the praises of the one he had acquired in Venice, I spoke with an importer and discovered he already had several in his warehouse here in Edinburgh."

Isabella sighed contentedly. "Is the kitchen close?" she asked, noting a separate door in the back corner.

"The kitchen is at the back of the house, through that door, as are the servants' quarters. There are rooms for four," he said, waggling his brows.

Although they hadn't discussed staff, she knew a cook would be their first hire.

Back in the hall, Daniel said, "The study is over here..." he waved to an arched doorway. "Parlor is in here." He led her into a brightly lit room adjacent to the front door, its window one of those on the front of the house. "Needs a carpet of some sort," he murmured.

"I can sew in here," she murmured, rushing to the south-facing window. "There's so much light."

Daniel grinned as he watched her stroll the perimeter of the room. "You could, but... would you like to see the upstairs?"

She paused and directed a suspicious glance at him. "Of course," she replied, rushing out of the parlor and to the stairs.

"Careful," he warned. "I shouldn't want you tripping in your condition."

An iron railing curved up the outer wall of the turret and ended at a landing while the stairs continued to go up.

"What's up there?" she asked before she stepped into a corridor that ran the width of the house and ended at a small wall with a window looking south.

"Oh, that's merely a place from where we can look out on the city," he replied.

"I could sew there, too?" she guessed.

"Well, you could, but I saw to it you have your own room for your avocation." He led her to where another corridor went off at a right angle. There were doors to two rooms on the right and two on the left, and straight ahead was a door at the end of the corridor. He opened the first door on the right. "Your study, madame," he said, opening the door to reveal a room papered in a yellow floral pattern.

"Oh, it's perfect," she said, happy to see a rocking chair and her sewing basket were already in place, as was a drafting table.

"Am I to share this room with you?" she asked, trailing a hand along the edge of the table. Instead of its top sitting at an angle, the table top was flat.

"No. That's my old drafting table, but I think you can use it when cutting out fabrics, can you not?"

Her eyes lit with excitement. "I can, indeed." She had her arms around his shoulders to kiss him before he quite knew what was happening.

He chuckled and took her to the next room, where the door was already open and workmen were inside painting the walls. "The nursery," he said, before immediately going to the door at the end. "And our bedchamber."

Isabella gingerly stepped into the large space, her eyes round. "It's so large," she said, slowly turning to admire the moldings.

"It only seems that way because the furniture hasn't been moved in yet," he countered. He noticed she had stopped to stare at a door in one corner.

"That door leads to what's behind this door," he said, taking several steps back. He opened the adjacent door in the hallway to reveal a bathing chamber with a water closet, a cast iron bathing tub, and the piping for a shower bath.

"This is as big as the nursery," she commented in awe, her gaze darting about until she noticed the checkered tile floor.

"That's because I made sure all the walls match up and the windows are the same size," he explained. "The next door room is a guest bedchamber for now," he explained. He placed a hand on her rounded belly. "Future bedchamber for when this little one outgrows the nursery."

"You've thought of everything," she said, sighing contentedly. "When can we move in?"

"A few days," he replied. "I have some laborers hired to bring a dray cart with our furnishings." He watched as she seemed to study the floor with great interest. "What is it?" he asked.

"We can play chess naked in here."

He barked a laugh. "I'm not sure we could reach the pieces when we're in the tub."

Isabella gave a start. "Who said anything about being in the tub?" she countered, waggling her blonde brows as she grinned in delight.

Daniel chuckled before he visibly reddened. "You're serious?" he asked.

Grinning in delight, she said, "I have the reputation of a rogue to maintain, or have you already forgotten?"

Wrapping one arm around the back of her shoulders while the other moved to her middle, Daniel said, "Hard to forget when the evidence is so... evident," he teased, gently rubbing her rounded belly before pulling her into an embrace.

In response, he received a quick kick in the palm and another into his ribs. His eyes rounded in surprise. "Ow! Was... was that him?"

"I should hope so," she replied, grinning in delight. "Because if it's a her, I fear she's going be just like me."

He lifted a shoulder. "So we'll simply dress her in jonquil gowns and let her roll around in the dirt," he teased.

Another kick hit his palm, and Daniel chuckled. "I think she heard me."

Isabella scoffed. "You do realize that every time you're being kicked, I am, too," she complained, although a grin teased the corners of her lips.

"Apologies, my sweet. Mayhap a kiss will help put her—or him—to sleep?"

"I'm willing to try," she said. She stood on tiptoes to take his lips with hers.

Having gained some experience in the matter, Daniel knew exactly how to return the kiss.

AUTHOR NOTES

Scottish Baronial or Scots Baronial architecture

Developed by the architecture firm Peddie & Kinnear in the 1830s, Scots Baronial was an architectural style based on Gothic Revival. The forms and ornaments are reminiscent of Scottish castles built in the Late Middle Ages, the rooflines embellished with conical roofs, tourelles (small towers), and battlements, often atop an asymmetrical floor plan.

ABOUT THE AUTHOR

A self-described nerd and lover of science, Linda Rae spent many years as a published technical writer specializing in 3D graphics workstations, software and 3D animation (her movie credits include SHREK and SHREK 2). Mythology, immortality, and ancient Greece have been lifelong interests.

A fan of action-adventure movies, she can frequently be found at the local cinema. Although she no longer has any tropical fish, she does follow the San Jose Sharks. A member of Novelists, Inc. and Wyoming Writers, Inc., she makes her home in Cody, Wyoming.

For more information:
www.lindaraesande.com
Sign up for Linda Rae's newsletter:
Regency Romance with a Twist
For articles on research and travels, read Linda's Rae
blog:
Regency Romance with a Twist